Allan Ahlberg

Half a Pig

illustrated by

Jessica Ahlberg

CANDLEWICK PRESS
CAMBRIDGE, MASSACHUSETTS

First U.S. edition 2004

Library of Congress Cataloging-in-Publication Data
Ahlberg, Allan.
Half a pig / Allan Ahlberg ; illustrated by Jessica Ahlberg. — 1st U.S. ed.
p. cm.
Summary: Esmerelda the pig is jointly owned by kindly Mrs. Harbottle and her
nasty ex-husband, Mr. Harbottle, who wants to turn Esmerelda into sausages.
ISBN 0-7636-2373-3
[1. Pigs — Fiction. 2. Humorous stories.] I. Ahlberg, Jessica, ill. II. Title.
PZ7.A2688Hal 2004
[E] — dc22   2003055426

10 9 8 7 6 5 4 3 2 1

Printed in China

This book was typeset in Gill Sans MT Schoolbook.
The illustrations were done in watercolor, colored pencil, and ink.

Candlewick Press
2067 Massachusetts Avenue
Cambridge, Massachusetts 02140

visit us at www.candlewick.com

Introduction

Dear Boys and Girls, thank you for reading the first sentence of my book (or listening to it, perhaps). The first sentence is often the most difficult to think of, we writers find, whereas the second, as you can see (or hear), is usually much easier.

So, let's get going. You will be all excited, I am sure, to hear (or read) the story. It is an excellent one in my opinion, but then I would say that, wouldn't I. It certainly has lots of good words in it.

Words like these, for instance:

spoon
rope

sausage

hippopotamus
bucket
underpants.

There are some running and
jumping words, like:

running and
jumping and
skipping and
tug-o-warring.

A little heap of useful "ands" and
"thes" and "buts" and so on.

but
the and
on as it
if and
of on the of and but
over of it at but of over
the if and but and as over
and as on of the

Some colours:

blue
brown
purplish
sausage-coloured.

Some noises (and groans):

Bang!

Splat!
Oooer!
Aaaargh!
Thump!

A few names:

Rose
Billy
Esmeralda
Slugger.

Some weather:

rain

showers and sunny intervals
cold front.

Some food (for a picnic perhaps,
but watch out for the rain[1]):

jelly
pizza
beans
cake
noodles
baked aubergine
swill.

Some good guys:

Rose and Billy (again)
Mrs Harbottle
Constable Murphy.

And ... some bad guys:

the Swiggins Brothers
the Swiggins Sisters
Mr Harbottle.

[1] and the hippopotamus

So there we are, plenty of words, I think you will agree, more than enough to make a good story with, and that's not all of them. I've just remembered another: "ghost" — that's a tremendous word. And "flabbergasting", that's a beauty — one of my favourites.

Anyway, let's see how we get on. I'll make a start, shall I? Are you ready? Really? Sitting comfortably and all that? Are you *sure*? Right. Here — we — go.

Half a Pig

Once upon a time there was
a little brown pig named Esmeralda.
Esmeralda was a contented pig.
  She loved her lovely bucket of
swill in the morning.

She loved the neighbours' children,
who came to talk to her and
scratch her back with a stick.

She loved the weather[2],
and the flowers in the fields,

[2] showers and sunny intervals

and the birds along the fences, and
even the flapping washing on the line.

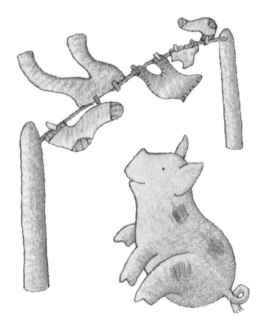

She loved her lovely bucket of
swill in the evening. Best of all,
she loved Mrs Harbottle.

Esmeralda lived with Mrs Harbottle
who, sad to say, owned only half of her.

Mr Harbottle owned the other half. Now that he and Mrs Harbottle were divorced, Mr Harbottle wanted his half.

Mr Harbottle was a horrid man with uncombed hair and dirty fingernails. All he ever ate was *sausages*. He had eaten so many that really he looked like a sausage, a sausage with a hat on … and a bristly chin.

Mr Harbottle came one day and banged on the door.

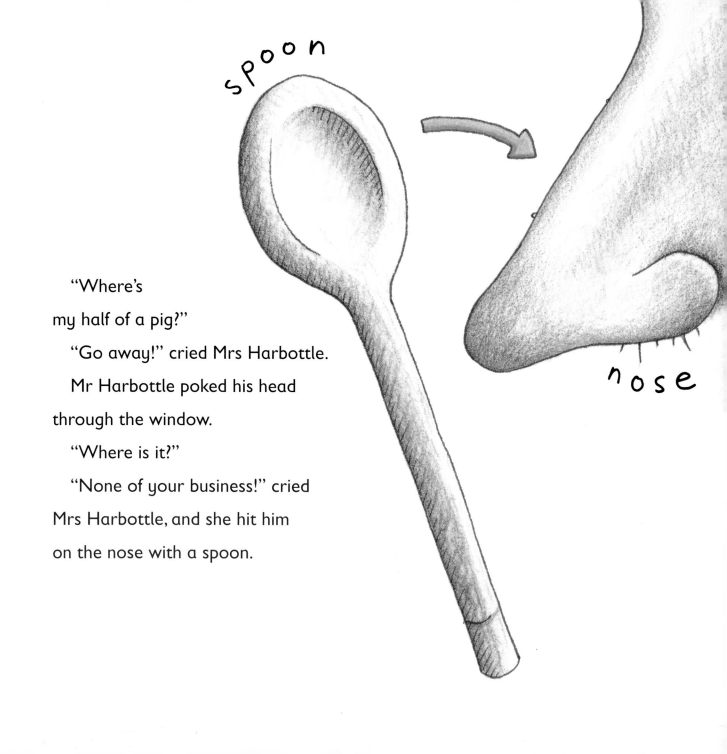

spoon

nose

"Where's my half of a pig?"

"Go away!" cried Mrs Harbottle.

Mr Harbottle poked his head through the window.

"Where is it?"

"None of your business!" cried Mrs Harbottle, and she hit him on the nose with a spoon.

In the afternoon, Rose and Billy, the children from next door, came round and talked to Esmeralda and scratched her back with a stick. Later on they found Mrs Harbottle crying in the kitchen.

"What are you crying for, Mrs Harbottle?" said Billy.

And Mrs Harbottle told him … and cried some more.

"It's sausages!" she sobbed. "That's all he sees in Esmeralda. That dreadful man – no sympathetic feelings at all."

Mrs Harbottle shook like a sad jelly in her easy chair. "Can't think what I ever saw in him."

Rose and Billy patted her shoulders and made her a cup of tea.

That night the Swiggins Brothers came and banged on
the door and broke it down. They said Mr Harbottle had
sent them and where was his half of a pig.

Esmeralda was hiding upstairs under Mrs Harbottle's bed.
The brothers found her and prodded her out with a broom handle.
Esmeralda, who was slippery and quick, got away
from them and bolted down the stairs, out the
back and straight into the *pokey sack*
that the Swiggins Sisters had waiting for her.

Poor Mrs Harbottle, sitting on her front step in the moonlight (and her nightie), wondering what to do.

Poor Esmeralda, tied up in the pokey sack, bouncing about in the back of the brothers' van.

Bad Swiggins Brothers – and Sisters – doing Mr Harbottle's dirty work for him.

But *brave*, yes brave
Rose and Billy, on their
bikes now (still in their pyjamas)
and following the van.

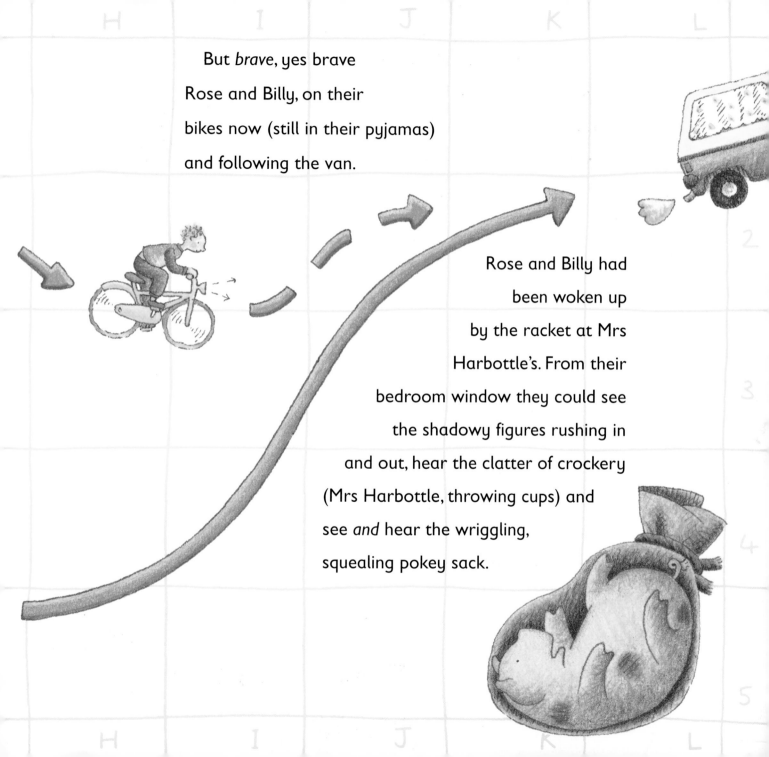

Rose and Billy had
been woken up
by the racket at Mrs
Harbottle's. From their
bedroom window they could see
the shadowy figures rushing in
and out, hear the clatter of crockery
(Mrs Harbottle, throwing cups) and
see *and* hear the wriggling,
squealing pokey sack.

 hedge

moon

owl

pig

shadow

The Swiggins Brothers in their van did not go far. Just through the village, dropping their sisters off at the Pig and Whistle, and out the other side to a deserted barn.

Rose and Billy left their bikes in the lane and hid in the hedge. Moonlight lay across the fields like floodlights at a football match. The barn door was open, a light flickering inside. An owl and its shadow swooped silently across the yard. A pig oinked.

whistle

oink

 dress

football

match

barn

Meanwhile Mrs Harbottle was drying her eyes and getting dressed. Mr Harbottle was just finishing a plate of sausages[3] in the Pig and Whistle. The Swiggins Sisters were leaning over his table whispering to him.

[3] with mashed potatoes and caramelized onion gravy

sausages

Inside the barn the brothers, Melvin and Roger,

had put together a small pigpen using some

wooden hurdles. Esmeralda had been released

into it and now the brothers were gazing at her and

scratching their heads. (While high up in the loft,

Rose and Billy were gazing at them.)

"What d'you reckon then, Rog?" said Melvin.

"Well it's half, innit," said Roger.

"I mean, 'half', that's what 'e said."

"Arh, but which half?"

Now the brothers were climbing into the pen[4].

Melvin grabbed Esmeralda while Roger took

a blue felt pen[4] from his pocket and drew

an untidy sort of line around her middle.

"Does that look like half to you?"

Melvin let go of Esmeralda

and put his glasses on.

"Hm … 'ard to say."

[4] A versatile word, "pen". It can also mean a female swan or an American prison. Fascinating.

Meanwhile Mrs Harbottle was
on the phone to Constable Murphy,
and Mr Harbottle had left the Pig and Whistle.

Furthermore, the weather was changing. A cold front was moving in and dark clouds were skimming the moon.

1

$\frac{1}{5}$ $\frac{3}{8}$ $\frac{6}{10}$ $\frac{3}{8}$

2

a
b
c
d
e

3

4

Back in the barn the perplexed brothers were seated now on sacks of fertilizer … pondering.

"We gotta do this properly, y'know," said Melvin.

"'Course we have."

"She's a good woman, that Mrs Harbottle."

"She is."

"Deserves her half as well."

"She does."

"Not three-eighths."

"No" – Roger was nodding his head – "nor seven-sixteenths neither." Melvin stood up and stared again at Esmeralda. "We could always weigh her, I suppose."

"Yeah," said Roger, and a thought occurred to him. "We could *mince* her." Whereupon there came a high-pitched, echoing scream from up in the rafters.

Noooooo!

A heavy bale of straw came tumbling down. It hit Roger on the shoulder, knocking him sideways into Melvin, who fell on and smashed one of the hurdles, releasing the imprisoned Esmeralda, who took to her trotters and ran.

Meanwhile Billy (the screamer) and Rose (the bale-thrower) were clambering back down the outside ladder. Mrs Harbottle was with Constable Murphy at the scene of the crime. *Mr* Harbottle was just opening the barn door.

Esmeralda seized her chance. As the door swung open, she charged into the gap, landing Mr Harbottle a painful blow to his tummy. Down into the mud he fell – it was raining now – only to be trampled on as he was struggling to his feet by the brothers as *they* charged out.

"Ah, Mr H!" cried Melvin. "How are y'sir?"

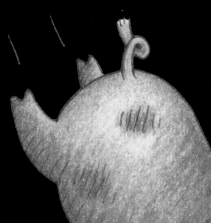

Mr Harbottle did not reply, partly because Melvin was still kneeling on him.

At this point (I almost forgot) a number of excellent words (and noises) now made their contribution to the story.

Thus:  **Bang!**

(Esmeralda colliding with Mr Harbottle)

 **Splat!**

(Mr Harbottle hitting the mud)

 **Thump!**

(Melvin landing on Mr Harbottle)  **Aaaargh!**

(Roger landing on Melvin)

Also, while I remember, "purplish", which Mr Harbottle's previously "sausage-coloured" face had become. Oh yes, and a little earlier, **Oooer!** from Roger in response to Billy's scream[5].

Actually, Mr Harbottle, I regret to say, made use of one or two other words at this time, which I don't believe your parents or teachers would wish you to hear (or read).

[5] He thought it was a ghost.

On with the story, or rather "chase", which is what it had now become. Esmeralda ran down the lane back towards the High Street, with Melvin, Roger and Mr Harbottle in pursuit, and Rose and Billy in pursuit of them.

A crowd of happy customers were leaving the Pig and Whistle, calling fond farewells to each other and opening their umbrellas.

"Stop that pig!" yelled Mr Harbottle. But Esmeralda skipped past them.

Esmeralda did *not* run into the Pig and Whistle, if that is what you were thinking. It would have made a good joke, I suppose, but there again pigs have little sense of humour. Besides, we writers must stick with the truth, and it never happened.

Instead Esmeralda darted down an alley and jumped over a gate. The chasing group (plus two or three adventurous young people from the pub) were close behind, slipping now and then in the wet conditions, blundering in the darkness. Mr Harbottle, bruised and battered, was in the lead. Suddenly he stopped in his tracks and let out a muffled cry. "Ooh!"

Something wet and scary was wrapping itself around his head. It was only washing on a line, but Mr Harbottle was not to know that. Nor was Roger, right behind him, who caught a glimpse of this frightful, "flabbergasting" thing and thought he had seen a ghost again.

Meanwhile Esmeralda trotted purposefully along. Like the Pied (pig) Piper she led those villains (by the nose, as it were) straight and true, across a couple of gardens, in and out of a clump of nettles, back at last full circle to her own home patch, her own dear owner and the strong arms of the law[6].

Constable Murphy was sharing an umbrella with Mrs Harbottle as they stood out in the garden looking for clues.

[6] Yes, I know, "straight and true" and "full circle", but somehow it feels right.

Suddenly, bursting into view in the light from the kitchen window and the constable's torch, came Esmeralda, closely followed, it seemed, by some kind of mad mud man with a pair of underpants on his head.

Mrs Harbottle was overjoyed to see Esmeralda, and vice versa. She fell to her knees and cuddled that little pig with no regard for the mud which transferred itself to her or the rain which was still falling.

Mr Harbottle and the Swiggins Brothers stood gasping and steaming in the torchlight. Any thoughts of escape were dashed by the presence of Constable Murphy's dog, who was watching them closely.

As he recovered his wits, Mr Harbottle tried to talk his way out of things. "We have done nothing wrong, officer," he said. "Just out for a little stroll, me and my friends here."

"Yeah, friends," said Melvin.

"We happened to come upon this pig," continued Mr Harbottle.

"And sort of … chased it like," said Roger.

"But only to return it to its rightful *half* owner," concluded Mr Harbottle.

"A likely story," said Constable Murphy (I think he meant *un*likely), and he gazed protectively at Mrs Harbottle. "I know who I'd believe."

"Ah, yes officer, but you see – *it's only her word[7] against mine.*"

"No witnesses," added Melvin cheerfully.

"No proof!" cried Roger.

Whereupon up spoke Rose and Billy. There *were* witnesses –

"Hurray!" cried one of the young men from the pub.

Rose and Billy were witnesses.

They had witnessed it all.

And as for proof …

[7] There's a *really* good word!

"Look at that blue line there!" cried Rose.
"Round Esmeralda's middle. He drew that!"
"No I never," said Roger.
"Yes you did. You were going to chop
poor Esmeralda up!"

"It's a lie!" "Oh, no!" cried Melvin
and Mrs Harbottle together.
"They were gonna *mince* 'er," added Billy.
"Shame!" cried the same young man from the pub.
Constable Murphy crouched down and
shone his torch on Esmeralda's tummy.
The incriminating line was
plain to see.

"Must've been waterproof, that pen,"
muttered Melvin, as he was being handcuffed
to his brother.

Mr Harbottle, meanwhile, had taken a step or two backwards with
the thought perhaps of making a run for it. A growl from the
constable's dog persuaded him otherwise. The dog's name, by the
way (maybe you worked it out?), was Slugger.

So here we are, almost at the end.
There's just the food, I think, the tug-o-war,
a bit more weather, and that should be about it.

A few days later Mrs Harbottle made a picnic for Rose and Billy as a reward for all their bravery and cleverness. It had most of their favourite foods in it — pizza, beans, jelly and so on. And the weather was fine. A ridge of high pressure covered the country and the sun shone down from a cloudless sky.

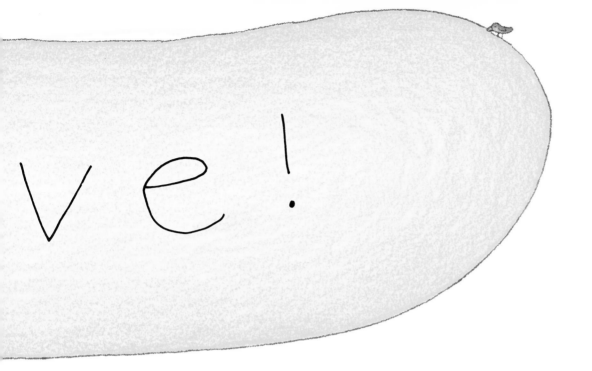

ve !

Across the river a crowd was watching the Annual
Pig and Whistle Charity Tug-o-war: ladies versus gentlemen.
The Swiggins Brothers, out on bail, were heaving away,
and the Swiggins Sisters too. Of Mr Harbottle there was
no sign.

But let's forget about him, and them. Back to the picnic.

Esmeralda was there, crunching daintily on a turnip. And,
surprisingly perhaps (or perhaps not), Constable Murphy was
also there, looking rather dashing in jeans and a checked shirt.
(It was his day off.) For that matter, Mrs Harbottle looked charming
too, in a pretty pale-green dress and plum-coloured cardigan.

"Would you care for a slice of angel cake, Shaun?"
said Mrs Harbottle.
"Thank you, Daphne, that would be delightful,"
said Constable Murphy.
And he smiled shyly.
And … so did she.

Conclusion

I know, I forgot the baked aubergine and the noodles – not really picnic food, are they? And the rope – I thought it might come in handy. And worst of all, the hippopotamus! I must have been mad (or overconfident at least). There's obviously no place for a hippopotamus in a story like this. There again, in some *other* story…

Have *you* ever thought of writing a story? Hm? It can be great fun, you know. Really. All you need is a pen, a bit of paper and a few words. Words like **rope**, for instance, **noodles** maybe, and **hippo- pota- mus.**

The End